# The Cat's Meow

## An Alex Quest Story

### BY BRUCE EHALT

illustrations
by Colleen Muske

## A KEEN EDITIONS BOOK

Dedicated to my parents, Rosemarie and Greg Ehalt

Copyright © 2013 Bruce Ehalt
The Cat's Meow, An Alex Quest Story
Published by Keen Editions
Printed in Canada
All rights reserved
First Edition

ISBN 978-0-9846603-4-6 (pbk)

This book was edited & designed by Ann K. Ryan
of Keen Editions, an independent Minnesota press.
Visit us at keeneditions.com and on facebook.

"Mom, do you know why cats say meow?"

"I don't," said Mom, "but that's a good question."

"Maybe I'll google it," Alex said.

"You could, but I have another idea. I bet Miss Tabby knows. She's a librarian and she loves cats. Why don't you and your little sister go next door and ask her."

T KATNIP
333 FUR LN

"Miss Tabby, Miss Tabby, we have a question for you,"
said Sun before Alex could even open his mouth.

"Good morning, Sun and Alex," said Miss Tabby.
"What can I do for you?"

"I was wondering," Alex rushed in, "why cats say
meow. We thought you might know the answer."

"I *do* know," said Miss Tabby. "Why don't you come in
and I'll tell you a story."

Alex and Sun had to move four large cats and one gigantic ball of yarn in order to find a place to sit.

MILK

"Would you like some tuna fish cookies and milk?" asked Miss Tabby.

"No thank you!" said Alex.

"Very well," said Miss Tabby. "Now I will tell you a tale."

**A long time ago,** in a land far, far away, there was a place named Feline.

The people there were hardworking folks. One thing that set Feline apart from all the other lands around them was that instead of an emperor, they had an empress.

**IN FELINE,** cats were everywhere. There were cats in the street, cats in the market and cats on the fishing dock. Every house had at least one cat. They were everywhere! They chased birds, and played and slept wherever they wanted. When they were asked if they wanted fish, they all chimed in, "me, me, me."

**THE EMPRESS OF FELINE** had more cats than anyone.
She placed pillows in every room so her cats could catnap
whenever they wanted. She even made cat laws.

All carts and horses must stop for cats.

Cat dishes must always be full of fresh food and milk.

Cats may wander wherever they want.

**THIS WAS THE LAW** the cooks of the palace *really* didn't like, because it meant they could **never** shoo cats out of the kitchen. **Ever!**

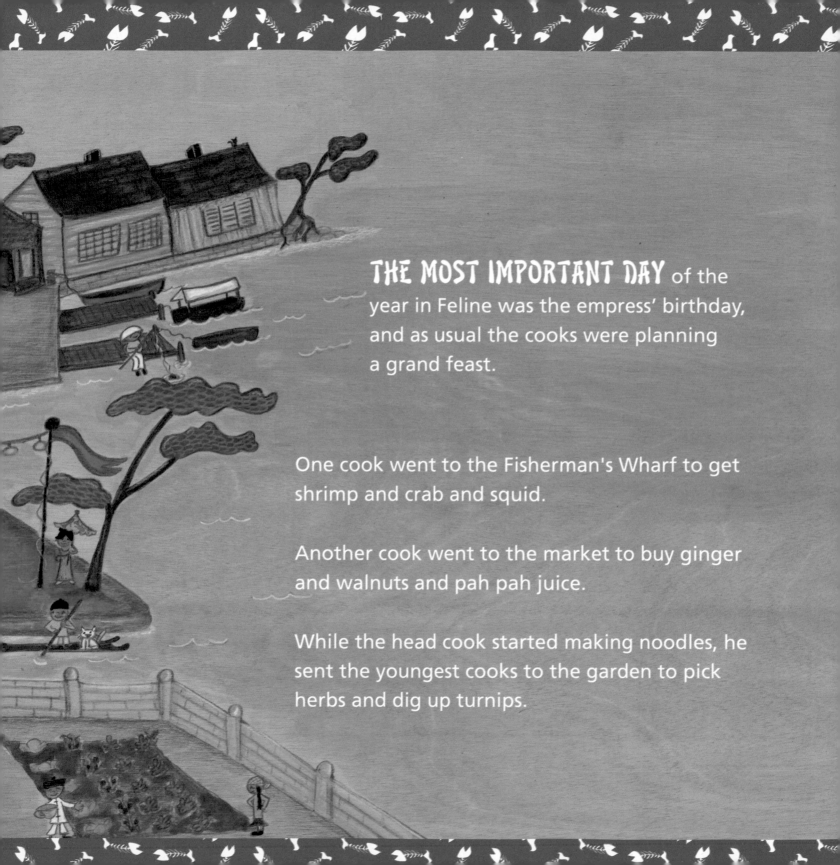

**THE MOST IMPORTANT DAY** of the year in Feline was the empress' birthday, and as usual the cooks were planning a grand feast.

One cook went to the Fisherman's Wharf to get shrimp and crab and squid.

Another cook went to the market to buy ginger and walnuts and pah pah juice.

While the head cook started making noodles, he sent the youngest cooks to the garden to pick herbs and dig up turnips.

**THE AROMAS OF** the feast filled the air and the palace cats crowded around the cooks.

ME

The head cook became very annoyed with the cats' constant cries of "me, me, me." To tempt them out of the kitchen, he hauled a big kettle of fish bones into the courtyard behind the palace.

"Here, kitty, kitty, kitty," he said. All the cats began to follow him. As he turned to open the kitchen door, he accidentally stepped on the tail of the biggest cat.

"YOW," said the cook.

"OW," said the big cat in response.

"OW OW OW," said all the other cats,
thinking this was a new game.

"ME-OW. ME-OW. ME-OW," said the big cat.
He liked the way this sounded.

"ME-OW. ME-OW. ME-OW," said all the other cats.
They liked this new sound, too!

**THAT NIGHT** at her birthday feast, just as the empress was blowing out the candles on her gigantic cake, all the cats started singing: "MEOW MEOW MEOW MEOW, MEOW MEOW MEOW MEOW." The empress clapped and asked for an encore.

**THE NEXT MORNING,** the empress called for the head cook to thank him for the marvelous feast. "The cat concert was a special treat!" she exclaimed. When the head cook explained how this came to be, the empress could see that the cook was not as fond of cats as she was.

"What shall I do?" thought the empress. She didn't want to banish the cats from the kitchen, but she needed to keep her cook happy, too.

"I know!" said the empress. "I'll make a new law just for the palace cats."

Palace cats must stay at least ONE tail's length away from the cooks.

**IN NO TIME AT ALL,** everyone in the palace kitchen
was happy. **Even** the head cook!

"One day we'll be famous for having the cleverest cats
in all the world!" he declared.

When Miss Tabby finished the tale, Alex asked,
"Is this a true story?"

"I like to *think* so," said Miss Tabby.

When they got home, Alex rushed to find Oscar.

"Have I got a story for you!"

# Learn along with Alex

In every Alex Quest Story, Alex learns about a different culture and a different time. In his quest to discover why cats say meow, Miss Tabby brings Alex and Sun back in time to a fictional place called Feline that is patterned after China's Song Dynasty. The Song Dynasty began around 960 and lasted for more than 300 years. It was a prosperous time, and a time of great discovery and innovation (including the magnetic compass for navigation at sea). *The Cat's Meow* is a great way for children to learn more about this ancient world, also known for its beautiful art. Help children find the details in the book's illustrations that point to these fun facts about the Song Dynasty!

## Printing

At the beginning of the Song Dynasty, people carved symbols in pieces of wood and covered them with ink to print words on pages. Each piece of wood could only be used to print that one page. In the 11th century, a man named Bi Sheng carved each symbol of the Chinese language on a small piece of moist clay. When the clay hardened, the pieces could be used over and over to make the symbols on any page. This was the beginning of movable type. Before this, very few books were printed. Movable type changed the whole world and helped more people learn to read because of all the books that were printed. Some books helped people study for tests that allowed them to get jobs. Books on farming and medicine were printed so people could have a better life. The first paper money in the world was printed in the Song Dynasty, too. Find the printer in the Feline market scene!

## Fireworks

Fireworks are another discovery of the Song Dynasty. For the first time, people used closed containers to shoot rockets into the sky. Rockets were used to entertain people at special celebrations throughout the year. Scientists remind us that this is the same idea as sending rockets to the moon! See the rocket fireworks in the birthday party scene!

## Art, Literature and Music

During the Song Dynasty — called the Golden Age of Painting — landscape painting was developed. The painting in Miss Tabby's living room and the first scene of the Feline story are landscape paintings. They show how a scene looks from far away. Beautiful poems were written and recited during this time. Find the poet reciting a poem in the birthday party scene. Chinese opera was also popular. Whole families of actors and singers traveled throughout the land to perform operas. In this story, we have a chorus of cats in the birthday party scene!

## Tea and "China"

In the Song Dynasty, it was a popular ritual to drink tea out of beautiful, porcelain tea bowls. The way they developed porcelain is why we call dishes "china" today. It wasn't just people in the palaces who drank tea and used porcelain. Fine porcelain bowls were found in people's homes and in restaurants. Look for beautiful bowls all over the book!

# About the author & the story

Bruce Ehalt was born in Long Lake, MN. He studied at both St. John's University in Collegeville and the University of Minnesota. Bruce has taught school at the elementary level since 1999 and is currently a second grade teacher in a Minnesota school. *The Cat's Meow* is his first children's book. Bruce's Alex Quest stories reflect his own natural inquisitiveness, as well as his desire to bring the joy of creative learning to students everywhere. Each of Bruce's Alex Quest stories is carefully researched so that cultural elements are authentic to the time and place written about — leaving room for creative license, of course!